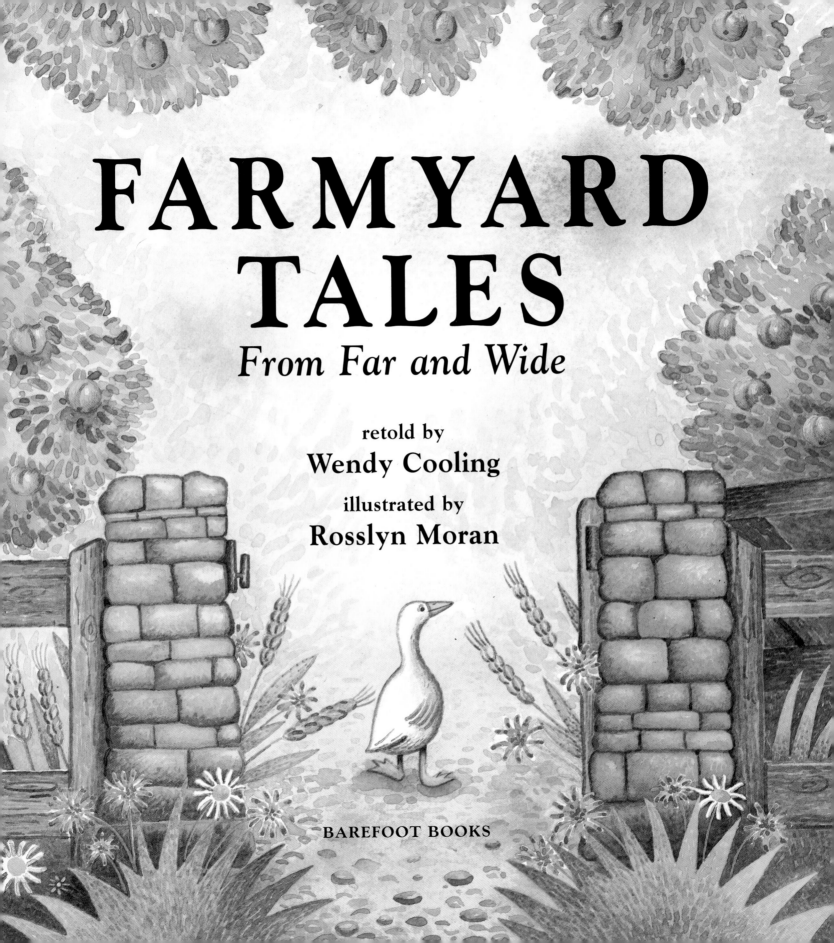

FARMYARD TALES

From Far and Wide

retold by
Wendy Cooling

illustrated by
Rosslyn Moran

BAREFOOT BOOKS

Contents

The Cock, the Mouse and the Little Red Hen

French

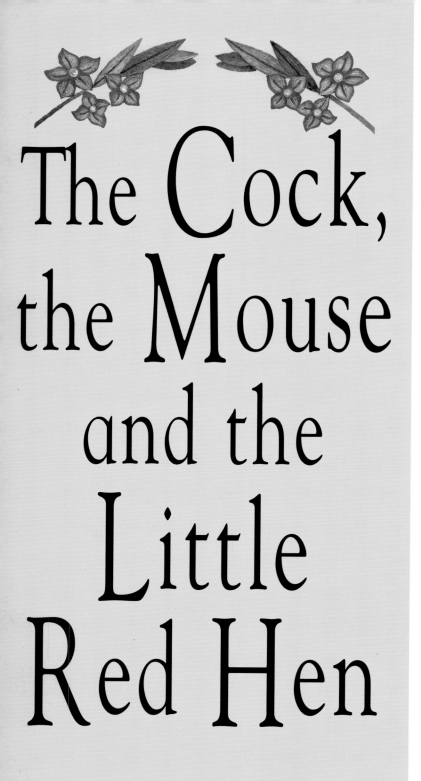

6

Once upon a time, a cock, a mouse and a little red hen shared a pretty house on the hill. Nearby, in an ugly house with peeling paint and a door that wouldn't close, lived bad old Mr Fox and four bad little foxes.

The little foxes woke up one morning feeling very hungry but there was no food in the house. "I'm so hungry, father," cried one little fox.

"We had nothing to eat yesterday," complained another.

"And no more than a mouthful of chicken the day before," moaned the third.

"And I can't remember having anything to eat the day before that," chimed in the fourth.

"Don't worry," said Mr Fox. "A cock lives in that little house over there."

"Yes," interrupted the little foxes, "and a mouse and a little red hen!"

"Right," said Mr Fox. "I'll take my sack and fetch that cock, that mouse and that little red hen. They're all nice and fat and will be good to eat. Make up the fire and put some water on to boil. Tonight we will have a delicious feast."

Now in the neat, green painted house on the hill, all was not well. The cock and the mouse were in the habit of being lazy. Today, they had both got out of bed on the wrong side, and were being very grumpy. They often let the little red hen do all the work and this morning they were even worse than usual.

"Who will gather sticks for the fire?" asked the little red hen.

"Not me!" said the cock.

"Not me!" said the mouse.

So the little red hen did it herself. She got the same answer when she asked for help with the breakfast and with all the other chores that needed to be done.

"Not me! Not me!" echoed round the house. So the little red hen bustled around working, while the lazy cock and the lazy mouse dozed.

Mr Fox crept up to the house. His loud knock at the door woke the cock and the mouse. "It's probably the postman," mumbled the mouse sleepily, opening the door. In pounced Mr Fox. He grabbed the mouse and dropped him into the sack. The cock only had time to call, "Doodle-doodle-doo," before he was pushed into the sack.

The little red hen came running to see what all the noise was about. She too was grabbed by cruel Mr Fox. He tied the sack tightly and set off home. The friends bumped up and down on Mr Fox's back. It was very uncomfortable and they felt miserable. Realizing that they were all in great danger of being eaten by Mr Fox made the cock and the mouse sorry for their lazy habits and grumpy manners. They were really very fond of the little red hen, and now they said they were sorry.

"It's never too late to change," she said, for she had a plan. She always kept her sewing bag tucked under her wing while doing her work, and in it she had a pair of scissors, a thimble, and a needle and thread.

Soon, Mr Fox stopped to rest under a tree and fell asleep. The little red hen heard his snores and swiftly got to work. With her scissors, she cut a hole in the sack so the mouse could run out. "Go quickly," she said to him, "find a stone just your size and bring it back here."

Then the little red hen snipped and snipped until the hole was big enough for the cock to escape. "Go," she told him, "find a stone as large as you are and bring it back here."

When the friends returned, the mouse pushed his stone into the sack and the cock did the same. The little red hen had also freed herself, and now she pushed a third stone into the sack. Then she put on her thimble, threaded her needle, and sewed up the hole as quickly as she could. Mr Fox began to stir and the cock, the mouse and the little red hen fled all the way home.

Mr Fox woke, picked up his sack and went on his way. The sack seemed heavier than ever to him. Then, as he crossed the stream, he stumbled, and the heavy sack pulled him after it into the water. Down and down he was dragged into the deepest of pools. Shoals of fish saw him and carried him away. He was never seen again. The four bad little foxes went to bed very hungry that night.

When they got home, the cock and the mouse turned over a new leaf. They lit the fire and did all the chores and let the little red hen rest in the most comfortable armchair. The friends were never troubled again by bad foxes and they still live together happily in the neat little house on the hill.

The Straw Ox

Ukrainian

L ong ago, a poor man and his wife struggled to make a living on a small farm. The man worked hard in the fields from sunrise to sunset and his wife worked hard at home spinning flax into cloth. They earned very little and finally the day came when they had no money to buy food for themselves. What was to become of them?

Suddenly, the old woman had a strange, but good, idea. "Go, husband," she said, "and make an ox. Make it out of straw and paint it with tar."

"I can't waste time doing that," said the old man. "What would you do with a straw ox?"

"Don't argue, just do as I say," replied his wife sharply. The old man liked a quiet life so he did as his wife asked.

The next morning, the old woman went out to the field to spin, driving

the straw ox in front of her to graze on the fresh grass. The sun was hot and the day was long and soon she drifted off to sleep.

A large, bad-tempered, brown bear came out of the forest looking for honey. He looked at the straw ox in amazement. "What are you?" he growled rather rudely.

"As you see, I am a straw ox, painted with tar," replied the ox.

"Good," said the bear. "Give me some tar to heal this wound on my leg." The ox didn't answer so the bear rushed at him and tried to bite off the tar with his teeth. But his teeth stuck and as he tried to use his paws to push away from the ox, they became stuck too! As he struggled to get free he pulled the ox back towards the forest.

Just at that moment, the old woman woke up and saw what was happening. She ran home shouting, "Husband, husband, a bear is stealing our ox! Come and help!"

The old man did as he was told. He caught the bear and locked him in the barn and then mended the poor ox.

The next day the woman led the straw ox out again and once more, as she tired of spinning, she drifted off to sleep. Now a wolf came out of the forest and questioned the ox. He too wanted tar, to cover his scratches made by thorns.

"Take what you need," said the ox. But as the wolf tried to do this, he too got stuck. As he struggled to get free, he pulled the ox along with him and was just disappearing into the forest as the old woman woke up.

Again she ran home shouting to her husband for help. The old man caught the wolf and locked him in the barn and then mended the ox.

The next day was the same, only this time it was a fox that ran out of the forest. He wanted tar to heal a wound made by hounds, but he too got stuck and dragged the ox away. Soon the fox was in the barn with the bear and the wolf.

On the fourth day, a hare became entangled in the straw and tar of the ox and ended up in the barn.

The old man wondered what he should do with the animals. The fur of the bear would make good, warm coats, he thought. Soon the bear heard the sound of a knife being sharpened. "Don't kill me," he pleaded. "Let me go and I will bring you honey every week."

Next the old man decided that the skin of the wolf would make caps to keep out the winter winds, but the wolf pleaded with him, "Let me live and I will lead a flock of sheep to your farm."

It was the fox's turn to worry as the old man continued to sharpen his knife, thinking that fox fur too would be warm. "Please let me live," cried the fox, "and I will bring geese to your farm and hens too."

That left only the hare whose skin would surely make warm mittens. "Please don't kill me," he cried to the old man. "Let me go and I will bring you jewels."

So the old man freed all the animals. His wife thought he was soft and was sure that the creatures would not keep their promises. But the next morning, there was a banging on the door and there was the bear with a hive full of honey. Next time the man looked out there was a flock of sheep in the yard and soon after, geese and hens appeared. Then came another knock at the door and there was the hare, almost collapsing under the weight of the riches he was carrying.

The couple could hardly believe their luck. From that day on they lived well and were happy. The straw ox grazed in the fields and slept in a warm stable. And the old man – he realized that he had an exceptionally clever wife.

Why Geese Don't Wear Boots

German

Once there was a small, very pretty goose who was extremely proud. She was especially proud of her small, delicate feet. She took great care to keep them very clean even in the worst winter weather. Often she stood with one leg tucked under the other so that at least one foot was kept warm as well as clean. She spent a lot of time thinking about her pretty feet and decided that the best way to keep them warm would be to wear boots - just like the children she watched skating on the pond and playing in the snow.

The little goose's mother did rather spoil her and so took her off to town to buy the pair of shiny, leather boots her daughter wanted so much. The little goose loved them as soon as she put them on and hurried straight home to play with the children and to show off

her boots. But how they laughed as she waddled over to join them, for she looked funny and a bit clumsy in her new boots. As soon as the little goose stepped onto the ice, she slipped and fell. She banged her head badly on the ice and had to be carried home.

Her mother was shocked to see the little goose arriving home hurt. She blamed it all on the

boots, for she knew really that boots were not meant for geese. The doctor came and sewed up the little goose's head and the poor creature spent many days in bed before she began to get better. But as spring arrived, she was ready to be up and about again and was happy to be out waddling with the other geese.

Now young geese have very short memories and soon the disaster of the shiny, leather boots was forgotten. When the little goose was out waddling one

morning in early summer, she saw a housemaid wearing a pair of beautiful red shoes. "They are just what I need," she said to herself. "Shoes like that will suit me so much better than boots."

Again the mother goose gave in. This time she ordered the boot-maker to make a pair of red shoes for her daughter. The little goose loved them. "They'll be great to swim in," she said. "And they will keep my pretty feet clean and dry."

Off went the little goose to the pond, showing off in her new red shoes. But oh dear! The shoes were so heavy that she couldn't swim in them. The ducks laughed at her, the frogs laughed at her and she was very cross to be seen looking so silly. Luckily the cook arrived, fished the little goose out of the pond and carried her home.

"I shall never go near that pond and those horrid ducks and frogs again," she cried. But soon the little goose was very bored with her own company and fed up with being at home. Mother goose took her shopping again and this time bought her a smart pair of green velvet slippers. Little goose was all set to show off again and was soon walking in the garden where the ducks and the frogs were sure to see her. She hadn't been as careful as geese need to be and hadn't noticed the hole in the garden fence, or the sly fox peeping through it. When she did, she turned to run away but lost her balance and slipped in her slippery slippers and fell. Now foxes are very fast movers and in a flash this fox reached her - one bite with his sharp teeth and the little goose was gone. There was nothing left of her but a few feathers and a pair of smart green velvet slippers.

Mother goose cried many tears for her proud little daughter. And the little goose's sad end was a strong warning to all the other geese, for some of them were nearly as proud as she was. They learned their lesson and since the day when the little goose in her green velvet slippers was eaten by the fox, geese have been happy to walk barefoot. Mother geese tell the story to any of their children who have a tendency for showing off, and no goose since has tried to wear boots, shoes, or slippers!

The Right Thing To Do

Indian

A flock of goats once grazed happily on the hillside all day long. The goats nibbled grass and wandered far and wide, but they knew they must always be home before dark. Towards the end of the day they always met together and made their way back to the village, sometimes with a young boy or girl to lead them and sometimes on their own.

There was one very old goat in the flock. Somehow she was always far away from the other goats as night fell and was always the last to get home. One day she was even slower than usual and was nowhere near the village when darkness came. She knew that wild and dangerous animals came out once it was dark and she was worried about spending the night in the open. As she thought and thought about the right thing to do, she noticed a cave in the hillside. "Yes," she said to

herself, "the right thing to do is to shelter in that cave until daylight."

It would of course have been the right thing to do if the cave had not been the home of a very fierce lion. Goats have a good sense of smell but this old goat was slow in every way and she didn't smell the lion until she could see him - and he could see her too. Again, the goat thought hard about the right thing to do. "I know," she decided, "I shall simply walk straight up to this lion, look him in the eye, show no fear and pretend I haven't noticed his powerful body, his sharp claws and his terrifying eyes. Yes, I'm sure that will be the right thing to do."

This time it really was the right thing to do. The lion had never been treated in such a way. Never before had any animal walked calmly into his den and looked him straight in the eye. Usually the animals he met, especially those much smaller than him, trembled with fear when they saw him and fled to escape his swift attack. The lion was too surprised to spring at the goat but just managed to roar, "Don't you know who I am? What are you doing in my cave?"

Thinking again about the right thing to do, the goat announced herself as the Queen of all Goats and said, "I am getting old and have promised myself that I will eat a hundred tigers, fifty elephants and twenty-five lions before I die. I have finished the tigers and the elephants and am ready to start on the lions."

Now saying this with confidence really was the right thing to do. The lion couldn't believe his ears; he was worried and even a bit afraid. But he was still a quick-thinking animal and asked the goat if he could go and wash in the river. He thought it was important that if you were going to die, to die clean. The goat thought the right thing to do was to let the lion go and so have the warm cave to herself for the night.

That would have been the right thing to do if the lion hadn't happened to meet a jackal as he was running from the cave. "Your hair's standing on end!" exclaimed the jackal, who had never seen a frightened lion before. "What on earth is going on?"

"Oh, oh," answered the lion, "I've seen such a goat, wild and horrible, said she was a queen. She was looking for lions to eat - she was going to eat me!"

This time it was the jackal who couldn't believe his ears. "It can't be true," he said. "It must be a trick. I'll come back to the cave with you - perhaps we can share that goat for dinner."

The lion and the jackal made their way quietly back to the cave. The goat hadn't managed to get to sleep and she heard them coming. "What," she wondered, "is the right thing to do now?" This time she had to think very quickly, for the lion and the jackal had mean and hungry faces. The right thing to do, she decided, was to show no fear or concern but instead to be angry. "Oh jackal, what is this?" she shouted. "You promised me twenty-five lions and all I can see is just one feeble one. You must be punished – I shall eat you both."

Imagine the lion's thoughts. He was sure the jackal had tricked him back to the cave. He was in a rage and roared the loudest of roars. That scared lion with hair standing on end turned into the fiercest, most terrifying of creatures. He sprang at the jackal, who ran out of the cave as fast as his legs would carry him. As the goat watched the lion chasing the jackal, the right thing to do became very clear. She left the cave and ran as fast as a goat of her age could run, all the way home. And that really was the right thing to do!

The Three Little Pigs

English

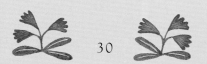

This is the story of three little pigs. These three little pigs lived a very ordinary life until one day their mother told them it was time for them to leave home and go out into the world. She gave them the sort of good advice mothers always give their children: "Now look after yourselves well," she said. "Build a good solid house. Keep yourselves clean and tidy and be sure to eat three good healthy meals every day. "And," she warned them, "always keep your eyes open and your ears sharp for that bad old wolf. I'm told that he prowls around people's houses these days. He likes nothing more than a tender young pig for his dinner."

Mother pig packed bundles of food for each little pig and waved them on their way, watching until they were out of sight.

The first little pig was rather lazy. He didn't like walking in the hot

sun and sat down to rest at the first farm he came to. He ate his lunch and looked around and his eyes settled on a large heap of straw. "That's it," he thought. "Just what I need if I'm to build a house." The farmer happily gave the pig some straw and soon the house was built.

The little pig was just settling down to his first cup of tea when there was a knock at the door. Then he heard the voice of the bad, old wolf, "Little pig, little pig, let me come in."

"Oh no," said the pig remembering his mother's warning. "Not by the hair of my chinny chin chin. I won't let you in."

"Then I'll huff and I'll puff and I'll blow your house in," called the wolf. And that is just what he did. He huffed and he puffed and he blew down the straw house and ate the first little pig for his lunch.

The second little pig walked a bit further and wondered what sort of a house he should build. By the time he reached the forest he too was tired. He ate his lunch and looked around. He saw lots of wood and decided that it would make him a good house. He built quickly and soon settled down to tea feeling very pleased with his work. The wolf of course was on the lookout for another good meal and was soon knocking at the second little pig's door. "Little pig, little pig, let me come in."

"Oh no," said the little pig who well remembered his mother's advice. He knew that wolves meant trouble. "Not by the hair of my chinny chin chin. I won't let you in."

"Then I'll huff and I'll puff and I'll blow your house in," said the wolf, and that's just what he did. He huffed and he puffed and blew down the wooden house and gobbled up the second little pig.

Now the third little pig had more sense than the others. He walked right to the next town thinking about the house he would build. He saw men building houses with bricks and saw that they were good and strong. A kindly builder gave him the bricks he needed and after many hours of hard work his house was built. It looked very smart and was strong enough to stand in the wildest of weather. This house certainly couldn't be blown down by any huffing and puffing wolf.

The third little pig sat happily in his comfortable house but before long there was a knock at the door and the big, bad wolf was calling, "Little pig, little pig, let me come in."

"Oh no," answered the pig. "Not by the hair of my chinny chin chin. I won't let you in."

The wolf huffed and puffed but he could not blow the brick house in. He grew very angry, for the huffing and puffing was hard work. He climbed up onto the roof and called, "I'm coming down the chimney. You can't escape!"

But the clever little pig was ready. He had a huge pot of water boiling on the fire. As soon as he heard the wolf coming down the chimney, he took the lid off the pot and the wolf fell right in. The little pig slammed the lid back on and that was the end of the big, bad wolf.

The third little pig is probably still living happily in his strong brick house just outside the town.

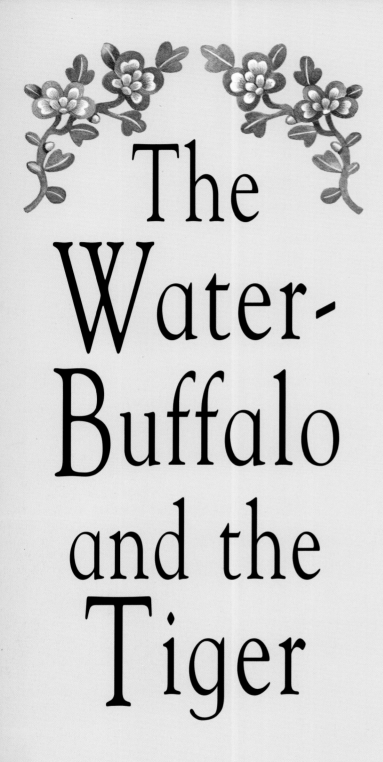

The Water-Buffalo and the Tiger

Chinese

Long ago, a farmer with his plow over his shoulder, led his water-buffalo to the fields to begin the day's work. The work was hard for the field was very muddy. Soon the water-buffalo was sinking into the soft, sticky mud. It was hard to move even one foot and even harder to pull the plow. It took him ages to plow a part of the field no larger than a plantain leaf.

The farmer was impatient and began to get angry. In his anger, he shouted at the water-buffalo and hit him hard with a stick. "You stupid animal," he screamed. "You're moving slower than a snail. Look at the tiger – why can't you be fast and strong like him?"

"What's so great about a tiger?" asked the water-buffalo as his master continued to beat and abuse him. But the farmer took no notice and continued to force the exhausted animal on through the field.

Now the water-buffalo was getting angry at the unfairness of it all. It was not his fault that the rain had been so heavy and made the field so muddy; he could think of no animal that could pull a plow faster through the deepening mud. "You think of me as a useless creature, do you?" he asked the farmer. "If you really believe that a tiger is a much better animal, take me to one tomorrow and I will prove you wrong."

The next morning, the farmer led the water-buffalo to the tiger's den. As soon as the tiger scented the water-buffalo he roared out to attack. Just as he was about to spring on him, the water-buffalo shook his sharp horns and spoke very calmly. "Tiger, I have not come here today to fight but to tell you that your teeth are blunt. Off you go and sharpen them for three days and I will sharpen my horns. Then we will fight."

The tiger roared his agreement and, back in his den, began to sharpen his teeth. He sharpened them for three days and three nights until they were as sharp as razors. The water-buffalo only spent one day sharpening his horns. He spent the rest of the time wrapping his body with layer after layer of straw. When his body was covered with a thick, padded layer he went for a good roll in the mud. Soon he was covered in black mud and the straw was invisible.

The day of the fight came and the water-buffalo returned to the tiger's den. The tiger was surprised by his appearance and asked, "Why on earth are you covered in mud?"

"It's midsummer," replied the water-buffalo. "I can't stand such heat. You know I like to have several mud baths every day."

The tiger examined the water-buffalo and thought that perhaps he had grown fatter over the three days. "Aha," he said, feeling even more confident of victory, "What a tasty meal I shall have today."

"Oh tiger, you may be able to bully animals like pigs and sheep, but just you wait – you won't be able to hurt me at all."

"I could have killed you three days ago," said the tiger, "but now that my teeth are like knives, my first bite will be deadly."

"Right. If you still think you're stronger, I'll lie down and let you bite me three times. Then you must let me butt you three times with my horns."

This seemed such a good offer that the tiger readily agreed and sprang at the water-buffalo. After three bites, the tiger was amazed to see his opponent unhurt. The tiger's teeth had torn the straw layers to shreds but there was not even a scratch on the water-buffalo. Then it was the water-buffalo's turn. He moved forward and butted the tiger three times, piercing him deeply with each butt until he fell down dead.

The farmer had watched all this in amazement and saw the wisdom and strength of his water-buffalo. From that day on he had respect for his animal and treated him well. Never again did he beat him or call him stupid.

To this very day, people respect water-buffaloes for their wisdom and strength and look after them well, although they can't plow as fast as horses or run with the speed of the deer.

41

One by One

Slovenian

Long ago, an old man said to his son, "You're growing up now, my boy. It's time for you to make your way in the world. There's no work and no money for you here so you must travel and seek your fortune."

The boy was sad and a little afraid of the great, wide world for he had always lived in the same homely village. But he knew he must do as his father said. So he packed a small bundle, taking just a few clothes and some apples and cheese for the journey and went on his way.

For many days the boy traveled but found no work. On the twentieth day he met a farmer, a very rich farmer, the owner of hundreds and hundreds of sheep and a great deal of land. He was looking for someone to look after his huge flock of sheep. The boy took the job and spent his days

walking the valleys and hillsides with the sheep and driving them to
fresh pastures. He was often many miles from the farm and it seemed
that the farmer owned the whole country. The boy was happy in his
work as he loved the fresh air and the peace of the countryside.

He was never lonely for the sheep were his friends. He stayed with
them as they gave birth to their lambs and watched as the lambs grew
into strong, healthy sheep. Often he slept in caves or took shelter
under hedges, only returning to the farm when his food ran low or
when it was time for the sheep to have their coats sheared, or for
them to be killed for meat. Sometimes, in the really bad weather of
midwinter, the boy would lead his sheep back to the safety of the
fields close to the farm where there was extra food in store. He was
very content with his life and soon forgot about the village where he
had spent his childhood.

One day his happy life was disturbed by a great storm that raged across the hills. The thunder and lightning seemed to come from all directions. The noise of the howling wind terrified the boy and the sheep. The wind pulled up trees by their roots and swept them through the valleys. The rain poured and seemed as if it would never stop – it filled the streams and rushed down the hillsides sweeping

bridges away as it went. Never before had the boy seen such a storm. He could scarcely stand upright in the wild gale, but he worked against the wind and the rain to gather the sheep together and to lead them to the safety of the farm. Still the storm beat against the land destroying all in its path.

By the time the boy and his bedraggled flock of sheep neared the farm there was only one bridge left. It was a ricketty old bridge made of worn wood and it looked as though it would be blown away by the next gust of wind.

The sides were broken and there was just one narrow plank of wood left across the fast-flowing river. The sheep could only cross one at a time. As the storm raged on the sheep began to cross the bridge to safety. One at a time they crossed and all the time the water in the river rose higher and swirled down the valley. The one plank shook and the sheep continued to cross one by one.

Now can you guess what happened next? The sheep continued to cross the bridge slowly and carefully - going just one at a time. Still there seemed to be hundreds of sheep to come. The plank creaked and cracked as each one crossed. One by one they went. One by one.

Remember, this really was the biggest flock of sheep the boy had ever seen - they still seemed to be coming down from the hills, each one looking more tired and wet than the one before. All the sheep in that flock that had once grazed in the hills and the valleys were trying to cross that collapsing old bridge one by one.

Would you like to know when all the sheep have crossed the river?

Well, the last I heard, they were still crossing that ricketty old bridge one by one. One by one.

Sources for the Stories

The Cock, the Mouse and the Little Red Hen

The origin of this story is unclear but we do know that similar stories have been told all over the world. The common idea in all the stories is the clever escape in which the heavy stones replace the imprisoned animal and trick the villain of the story into believing he still has his captives.

The Straw Ox

This story comes from the oral tradition of eastern Europe and western Asia – stories were often told by travelers to while away long evenings and so spread over thousands of miles. The story's theme of the magical arrival of wealth is popular in traditional stories all over the world. It has been told in many versions, in many countries, for hundreds of years. This is a version from the Ukraine, a country in which people have known poverty.

Why Geese Don't Wear Boots

There are many traditional stories that explain why various animals are as they are. This one comes from Germany and was originally told by Niedergesaess. It was retold by Sophie Hirch in her book *Friends Old and New – Twenty German Nursery and Fairy Tales*, published in 1900.

The Right Thing to Do

This Indian fable is told in many ways, sometimes about different animals and sometimes the jackal does not come into the story. The oldest version I found was "The Lion and the Goat" in *Indian Fables*, collected and edited by P. V. Ramaswami and published in 1887. This collector claims that the fable, an animal story of wisdom and trickery, originated in the East; some scholars disagree with him.

The Three Little Pigs

There are numerous versions of this well-loved English story that has been told to children for many generations. It is thought to have been first collected by Halliwell in the nineteenth century. J. J. Jacobs, a very famous scholar of folk and fairy tales, suggested that as pigs don't grow hair on their chins, the three animals in the story may originally have been goats.

The Water-Buffalo and the Tiger

This story, like many Chinese folk tales, is ancient in origin. It gives a glimpse of Chinese life and of the culture and traditions that date back over thousands of years. It is part of the oral tradition that has kept many of the stories alive through the ages. This tale was collected this century and published in Peking in 1958 by the Foreign Language Press.

One by One

This story from Slovenia follows the long tradition of European folk tales in which young men are sent out to find their own way in life: a necessity in many families. In folk tales the sons usually find happiness and often wealth. Stories of animals were important too as people often depended on their animals for survival. This is an unusual story because of its lack of resolution.

Barefoot Beginners — an imprint of Barefoot Books Ltd, PO Box 95, Kingswood, Bristol BS30 5BH, United Kingdom. Text copyright © 1998 by Wendy Cooling. Illustrations copyright © 1998 by Rosslyn Moran. The moral right of Wendy Cooling and Rosslyn Moran to be identified as the author and illustrator of this work has been asserted. ISBN: 1 901223 38 8

BAREFOOT BOOKS publishes high-quality picture books for children of all ages and specializes in the work of artists and writers from many cultures. If you have enjoyed this book and would like to receive a copy of our current catalogue, please contact our London office – tel: 011 44 171 704 6492 fax: 011 44 171 359 5798 email: sales@barefoot-books.com website: www.barefoot-books.com

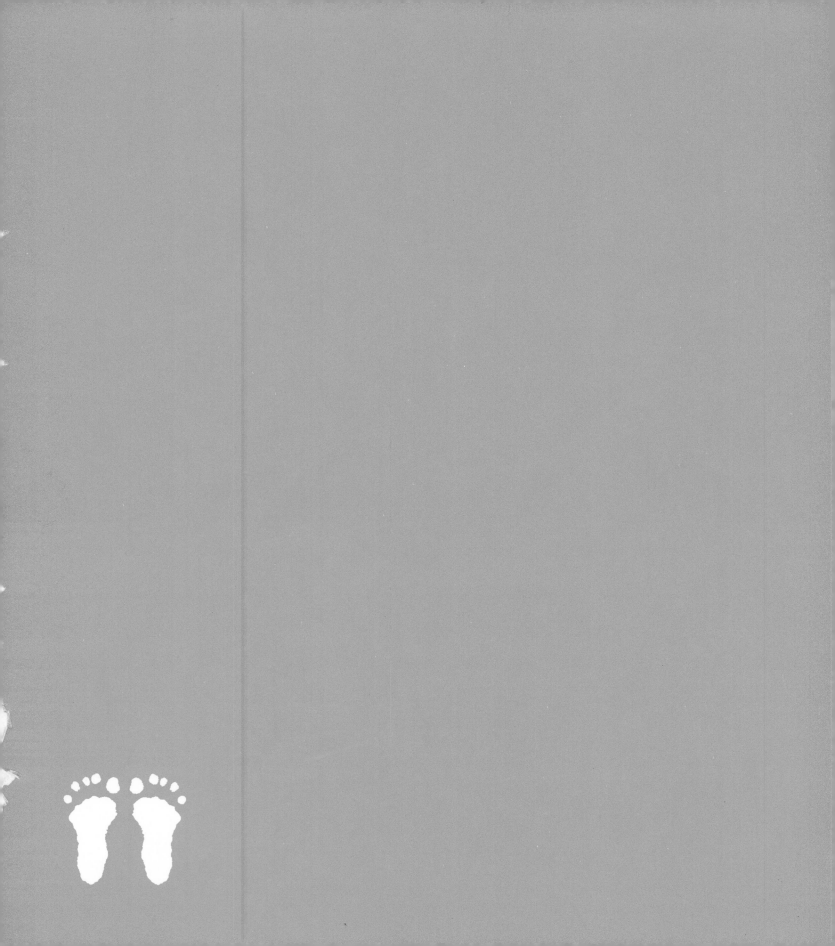